TEMPT
A TWISTED WOLF TALE

RENE FOLSOM

SYNOPSIS

Deep in the Shrouded Wood, on her way to her granny's cottage, Rosetta is ambushed by an unseen force. Soon after, she finds herself plagued by strange dreams—visions of a large wolf and a seductive woman beckoning her.

Not knowing what to do with these dreams and the odd changes happening to her body in the waking world, Rosetta sets out to confront whatever lies in the Shrouded Wood, determined to discover the temptations within. But what she finds is beyond anything she ever could've imagined... or hoped for.

Get ready to dive into Rosetta's world and enjoy a new twist on the classic tale of Little Red Riding Hood.

*This Halloween, something sinfully wicked is coming your way. Give yourself a Red Hot Treat this fall with ten spine-tingling stories sure to warm up your night. Scary just got sexy with **TEMPT**, part of the Red Hot Treats multi-author series (stands alone for reading enjoyment).*

First Edition. Printed in the United States of America.
ISBN-13: 978-1502730046 | ISBN-10: 1502730049

Editing Services Provided by:
Cynthia Shepp - www.CynthiaShepp.com

Cover Created by Phycel Designs
www.Phycel.com

For Michael Loring—
who inspired me to bring the wolves out to play.

†ABLE OF CONTENTS

†EMP†

THE MARK

This blows.

Puffing a lock of dark hair from my eyes, I made my way through the forest, bristling whenever my long, red cloak caught on a cluster of briars. I cursed under my breath as I used my empty wicker basket to swat them away. I worried that my favorite piece of clothing would get ripped during the trip. It being the only possession I had left of my father, I wore it obsessively when the weather began to cool, but I still managed to take great care of it. So, while picking my way along the overgrown path, I did my best to hug it close to my body as I walked.

My new, white Nike's crunched the dead leaves under my feet as I picked up my pace, the sound echoing off the bark of the trees surrounding every side of me. Looking around, my eyes took in the splendor of a forest overtaken by autumn and it immediately reminded me of my dad, who often complemented me on how beautiful my ocean-blue eyes looked against the colors of fall—a stark contrast, yet complementary all the same.

The leaves were a beautiful shade of yellowish orange—what was left of them anyway. As winter drew near, the trees began to shed their superfluous accessories and were padding up for the cold. I couldn't help but feel it a shame that they mostly littered the ground instead of living peacefully up on the branches above my head. Through the thicket of tree fingers, I could see the bright, blue sky overhead, a small whisper of a smile quirking my cheeks at the sight. Any other time of year, I'd be cast in complete darkness. So I couldn't complain too much about the pretty leaves falling down.

The beautiful sky didn't stop me from griping about having to be in the forest to begin with, though.

I loved my mother. I really did—honest. After my father passed when I was only eleven, my mother stepped up and took care of me all on her own. It was tough work, taking care of a young girl who had just lost her daddy, but my mother had done it fantastically. That being said, I couldn't help but question from time to time whether or not the duties had caused my mother to go slightly mad.

"Why else would she make me walk the entire way to Granny's house by myself?" I grumbled under my breath, talking aloud to help vent my frustration. "I could be with Cody right now…"

It sucked because I promised to spend the afternoon with my boyfriend, Cody. But, at the last possible second, my mother instructed me to make the ridiculously long trek to my grandmother's house. The old woman's cottage sat in the middle of the forest just on the outskirts of our humble little town. *Village is more like it*, I thought snidely.

I couldn't even borrow my mom's car to make the trip, which increased my annoyance even further. Even though I'd turned twenty-one this past June and had my license since I was seventeen, there was really no reason for me to have a car of my own while living in such a small town, especially when making a trip deep into the Shrouded Wood Forest where my grandmother lived. Being the old hermit that she was, she decided to live in the one house on earth that wasn't car accessible. So, instead of sitting in the soft, comfy seat of my mother's Honda, listening to instrumental rock music, I was waving around a silly wicker basket at all these damn briars that seemed to have it out for me. The basket was something my mom had made, a product of one of her most recent fly-by-night hobbies. So, I carried it around in support of her extracurricular endeavors. Thankfully, the wicker material was light as I stumbled through the nearly dead forest on a mission to collect my granny's special baked goods for the upcoming Halloween festival.

Why my mother had chosen to accept the position of Festival Director from the town committee was beyond me. She always managed to bite off more than she could chew. The title meant that she pretty much had to take care of *everything* for the Halloween festival, which meant I became my mother's delivery girl for two solid weeks prior to the event. Traveling from shop to shop, knocking on peoples' doors to ask for donations and other specific items they may or may not be able to contribute—such as designed banners, carved pumpkins, and a butt-load of candy—and now walking through the confounded forest to my granny's for her homemade truffles.

"This blows," I grunted as my red cloak once again caught on one of the many briars jutting out from the edge of the path.

Before I could stifle my little hissy fit, I heard my groans echoing off the never-ending tree line of the forest. Was that really what I sounded like? I needed to take a mental note to stop being such a ninny. After all, the errands I was being forced to do were only so the town could have fun, getting in the spirit of celebrating All Hallows Eve like a bunch of goons. Plus, I did enjoy spending time with Granny, despite the near-death experiences I had to endure just to get there.

Keeping quiet, I picked up my feet and continued, the brush getting a bit thicker with each step I took. The sound of crunching leaves beneath my feet had quieted a bit as I made my way into the last clearing before reaching Granny's front door. I still had a ways to go, but reaching the milestone gave me a bit of relief knowing I was making some sort of progress in this godforsaken forest.

Stopping abruptly, I listened. I knew I hadn't been grumbling or groaning about anything, but I heard that distinct sound again. Of course, I was aware there were some creepy crawlies out in the Shrouded Wood, but for me to be spooked during one of my midday treks to Granny's house was a bit foreign to me. I was usually pretty brave when it came to making my way through these woods, but whatever had made that noise sent chills down my spine.

While trying to keep as quiet as humanly possible, I took one step and then another, my heart thundering in my chest at the impression something, or someone, was watching me. I could feel the hairs stand up straight on the back of my neck—the kind of sensation you get when you knew someone was tracking your every move. I suddenly felt like a small rabbit being hunted by something much, much bigger than I was.

It had to have been my imagination. No one ever came this deep into the forest. No one, except for my grandmother's delivery guy, Billy, but he would've made his trip out here just a few days ago. We usually used him whenever we needed to get a message to Granny and his trips didn't often falter from their normal schedule.

Before my right foot found purchase against the ground dusted in the occasional leaf, I heard it. This time, it was a slight rustle of leaves, almost like footsteps, coming up behind me.

Taking a deep, fortifying breath, I willed myself to stay strong as I grabbed both sides of my hood and placed it calmly on my head, obscuring my face from the outside world. I contemplated whether to turn and see who was sneaking up on me. Did I want to face my attacker? No.

And god forbid any phones could possibly get signal out here. I knew it wasn't possible, so I'd left mine at home. But, the part of me that desperately needed the security blanket absentmindedly reached into my pocket for the contraption, cursing beneath my breath when I found it vacant.

Deciding not to look back—never look back—I began to speed-walk across the clearing, contemplating the idea of sprinting the rest of the way.

Don't be a coward, I repeated in my head while briskly walking toward the dense line of trees ahead. This time, I knew it wasn't my imagination. I heard—no, felt—the pounding footfalls behind me, the pattern oddly matching the erratic beat of my heart.

Yeah, fuck that! I thought as I busted out in a full-on sprint, throwing caution to the wind, and dropping the wicker basket so I had both hands to carry the hem of my cloak.

The heavy hood slowly fell back to my shoulders as my foot caught on some old roots, my body slamming to the ground in a heap of red. A yelp escaped me, the hard floor ripping the breath from my chest and my head hitting something with a loud thud.

For a second, all I could see was white. The blow had knocked all sense from me—both my breath and sight being difficult to grasp, as if they were tangible items just out of my reach. Once I regained my vision and very little of my composure, I gripped my forehead, my fingers coming away in a shaky, bloody mess, and I groaned in pain.

Looking up at the blue sky, I wondered how foolish I looked to the forest critters around me.

Then, the bare tendrils of the tree line began to shudder.

They looked as if they were dark, trembling fingers coming to pick me up, take me away.

I felt faint.

The last thing I recall seeing before the beautiful, blue sky went black…

A pair of fierce, golden eyes.

The Warning

The smell of chocolate assaulted my senses, and the warmth of the sun beat against my eyelids. Coughing, I turned and cracked open one eye to assess my surroundings.

Plush, green grass with a sprinkle of autumn wildflowers filled my vision, the top layer of blades haphazardly peppered with dry leaves. The late-afternoon sun pelted the side of my face, but I knew that couldn't be right. Or could it?

I was headed out to Granny's shortly after lunch. There was no way I'd lost several hours wandering the woods. Or was there?

Then it dawned on me—I was no longer in the clearing. I was now in front of my granny's house, the smell of her chocolate truffles wafting out through the windows and assaulting my overly delicate sense of smell.

With caution, I sat up, wincing at the pain radiating through my chest and up into my head. Reacting quickly, I touched my forehead with my fingers and felt the growing welt. It was no longer bleeding, but it would be one hell of a bump for a while. *Cody will find that attractive,* I thought absentmindedly. Looking around, I noticed my wicker basket sitting upright only a few feet away from my prone body—odd, considering I had dropped it back in the clearing.

"What the hell happened to me?" I said in a near whisper, looking down at my untattered, almost pristine clothing. If I had subconsciously dragged my injured ass to Granny's house, surely I would've shredded my cloak in some way. The brush only increased in thickness the closer the path came to her yard. But, it was in perfect condition, almost as if I'd floated here or something.

"Rosetta, darling!" Granny yelled from her door only a few yards away from where I still sat in the grass, dumbfounded. "What are you doing out there on the ground? Come in."

"Coming, Gran," I shouted back. My voice lacked conviction as I contemplated what the hell had gone on in the woods.

A burning sensation had me gasping for air, bringing my attention to my chest as if something had gotten into my cloak. Pulling away the lapel, I took a sharp, deep breath as I noticed scratch marks covering my heart.

Three neat scratches.

As soon as my eyes landed on the injury, the pain began to wane and a new tingling sensation sent my heartbeat into overdrive. The sensation felt so good, and I couldn't even explain why it was suddenly... attractive to me. I couldn't get myself to stop staring. The idea of tearing my eyes away from the beautiful markings just seemed... wrong.

"Rosetta?" Granny questioned, poking her head out the window this time and getting my attention.

Embarrassed, I immediately covered up the scratches and hauled my butt up from the ground, scooping up the basket on my way to the door. "Coming!" I shouted, mentally preparing myself for the barrage of questions Gran would surely throw at me once she saw my head.

Once inside, I took a moment to breathe in the wonderful scents of baked goods coming from the kitchen to help ease my anxiety. I felt frazzled, foggy. After a few deep breaths laced with the delicious smell of sweet chocolate, I felt a bit better. Not to mention the strange tingling was still radiating throughout my chest, stirring warmth in my belly and calming me to a degree.

It felt... nice... pleasant.

"Granny?" I called out, stepping further into the cottage. My grandmother had never been a person to be enticed by material goods, and her home mirrored that sentiment. Modestly sized, the cottage was all living room and kitchen with a smallish bedroom pushed off to the back. She was by no means in any financial dilemmas, making a pretty enough penny by selling special herbs and plants that grew indigenously in the Shrouded Wood, but instead of buying a sixty-inch television and a massage chair, she mostly just bought ingredients for the many cooked delicacies she was famous for around town. The only thing she ever splurged on was a moderately sized TV that was more for me during my visits than for herself.

"In the kitchen, dear!" Granny called back.

Feeling a bit more like myself in this familiar place I liked to call my second home, I made my way into the kitchen, smiling faintly at the sight of my grandma in her natural element. She was hunched slightly over, balling up more cake batter as chocolate melted on the stove—all ingredients that would make another batch of her delicious truffles, soon to join the four dozen or so others that were cooling off on the table. I could smell she had more cake baking in the oven and smiled at the fact I would get to stay and help her for a while.

"Hey, Gran," I greeted, placing my basket on the table next to the cooling truffles. "Hard at work, I see."

She turned to me, smiling warmly for a second before she got a good look at me. Her face instantly became etched with worry.

"Rosetta!" She scurried over, her tired body barely able to keep up with her young, vibrant spirit. She may not have the same energy she had twenty years ago, but she was still as spry as a woman half her age. "What happened to you?"

I knew the questions were going to come. The growing welt on my forehead was way too noticeable to hope no one would notice. Not to mention the damn thing throbbed, making it feel more like the size of a watermelon rather than a golf ball.

"I just fell, Granny," I said, not sure what else to say and embarrassed of the fuss she'd surely make. I *had* fallen, hadn't I? It was what happened afterwards that I was fuzzy on. "Hit my head on a rock."

"Oh, poor darling," she cooed. "Let me get something to help with that."

"Oh, no, I'm fine… really—"

"Hush," she said, waving her hand in my face as she scurried off to her room where she kept all of her special herbs and ointments. She was a firm believer in all that New Age stuff that I didn't fully understand. She partook in a few of the practices from time to time—such as trying to read my palm, trying to find meaning in the constellations, and trying to use divination to ascertain the location of lost items. Keyword being *trying* in all instances.

"This," she announced as she reentered the kitchen, brandishing a small bottle of greenish yellow gel, "is a salve taken from the Comfrey leaf. It's perfect for taking care of bruises, cuts, and arthritis aches." She lifted the bottle and gave me a toothy grin. "Trust me, it works."

I raised a brow at her. "Is that why you keep throwing out your arthritis meds?"

She waved her hand in my face again. "As I was saying," she said, completely ignoring my question while popping the lid off the bottle. "With this salve, your cut will be gone in no time at all." She gestured for me to sit in one of the kitchen chairs. I had just sat down as she continued, "It will help you stay nice and pretty for your little boyfriend there back in town."

She winked at me, and I couldn't help but blush.

"Granny..." I whined.

"Sit still while I work my magic," she instructed with a playful lilt to her voice, dabbing her finger into the greenish goop and gently spreading it over the cut on my forehead. I scrunched my nose up as the smell assaulted me.

"Ugh," I grunted. "That smells like rot."

"It's not the smell that matters, sweetheart," Granny said sagely. "It's the effect that does."

I sighed, but said nothing else as she continued to apply the medicine to my wound.

"There." She smiled, pulling back to admire her work. "Before you know it, there will be no trace of a cut having been there at all. Plus, your skin will be as smooth as a baby's bottom, I guarantee it."

I just gave a chuckle, unable to resist the affect my granny's cheerful demeanor had on others around her. She was such a bubbly, happy woman. There was no question in my mind that I loved her dearly.

"Thanks, Gran," I said, standing up. I reached to touch the salve to test its texture, but my hand was slapped away before I could even get near it. "Ow!"

"Don't be poking at it, young missy," she said sternly. "You might rub it off, and you'll be stuck with that wound on your—"

During her lighthearted scolding, she jabbed me in the chest with her bony finger, unknowingly poking one of the scratches under my lapel. I winced, and she paused to stare at me in confusion.

"Rosetta?" She tilted her head, concern etching her once-joyful face. "Are you okay?"

I quickly covered up my discomfort, forcing a light smile to shape my mouth. "Yes, I'm perfectly fine."

She pursed her lips together and stared at me hard. I knew that face all too well, and unconsciously shifted under her stare, giving her all the reassurance she needed that I was lying.

"Let me see," she demanded. "I know bull hockey when I hear it."

"Granny, please—" I tried to say, but she quickly reached forward and pulled aside my lapel to expose the three neat scratches branded onto my chest.

"Dear Lord!" she exclaimed, her eyes bulging at the sight of my mysterious wounds. "What happened to you?"

I hesitated for a second before answering, "I... fell..."

"You don't get scratches like these from being clumsy, Rosetta," she said, hardening her gaze at me. She knew I was lying and wasn't the least bit pleased with what she was witnessing.

Ignoring her concerned stare, I looked down and examined my wound, tracing a finger lightly over the beautiful patterns. It was as if everything happening around me disappeared, and I was transplanted back into the woods, wishing, yearning, for something... or someone.

The pleasant feeling of desire replaced my discomfort, and I smiled, closing my eyes and just enjoying the sense of belonging.

The smell of burning chocolate brought me out of my reverie, my eyes snapping open at the realization Granny was still staring at me in disbelief. In an attempt to disregard her scolding gaze, I hopped up from the kitchen chair and went over to the stove, turning down the heat and stirring the melted chocolate like it took all my concentration to do so.

"Oh, dear," she whispered behind my back, worry evident in her tone. At that moment, I couldn't stand to look at her. I knew she would make more out of this than deemed necessary. Her imagination was a wild one and usually meant I would be in for a long, drawn-out story involving the majestic creatures that called this forest home.

But this time, I didn't want to hear it. This time, it seemed so much more personal to me, like I needed to protect this particular part of me. I didn't have any idea why I felt so defensive, but I imagined only time to figure out my feelings would give me answers.

"Did you put in the secret ingredient yet?" I asked in an attempt to change the subject.

"Rosetta," she said, trying to get my attention. Her voice was getting closer, telling me she was approaching me from behind.

"I can help you coat this next batch. Is the chocolate ready?" I asked again, just dying for her to drop it.

"Rose, look at me," she demanded, her voice now directly over my shoulder. A warm hand touching my forearm had me whipping around, my defensive stance startling both of us.

"Gran. Is. The. Chocolate. Ready?" I said again, my voice coming out in pants this time.

The startled look on her face as she covered a gasp with her old, wrinkled fingers was more than I could bear. I felt horrible for scaring her. After all, it wasn't her fault my klutziness got the better of me.

"I'm sorry," I said with a deep exhale as I closed my eyes, trying to calm myself, wishing she would hear the sincerity in my words. "I'm just embarrassed about being so clumsy. Can we just drop it so I can help you get on with these truffles? They smell delicious."

"Like I said, Rose... those scratches aren't a product of clumsiness," she said, pausing as she braced herself on the counter next to me and continued rounding the cake balls. "And, yes, the chocolate is ready. Can you lay out some more wax paper for me?"

For the next several minutes, we silently busied ourselves with making the truffles. I even snuck a few samples here and there. The chocolate hitting my tongue had my eyes nearly rolling in the back of my head—sweetness exploding on my taste buds and making me moan with the exquisite flavor. To this day, Granny refused to reveal what her secret ingredient was, but there was something she added to the chocolate coating that made her truffles stand apart from any other I had ever tried.

"I can tell you don't want to talk about it, but I don't give a flying hoot what you want. This needs to be said," she deadpanned, her hands coming to halt as she turned to face me.

"Really, Gran, I'm fi—"

"Don't you dare say you're fine," she scolded, cutting me off mid-sentence. Of course, the old woman could tell exactly what I was going to say before the words spilled from my mouth. I sometimes wondered if she were clairvoyant.

Grabbing my hands, she wiped the chocolate off my fingers with a towel and led me over to the kitchen table, arranging the chairs so I was forced to face her, our knees nearly touching. I cringed as she pulled my lapel aside, not out of pain, but out of fear she would judge me too harshly—judge something that ultimately didn't even concern her.

"Everything about you concerns me," she blurted. Had I said that out loud?

"It's nothing. I can't even feel it anymore," I explained, pulling away marginally so she wouldn't touch it. "Don't worry."

"That's crap, Rose, and you know it. I know you can still feel it," she said, pulling away and allowing my cloak to cover my chest again. "You feel pleasure, don't you?"

"Granny," I said, looking everywhere but at her as my face turned fifty shades of crimson.

"You know what I mean. The wound doesn't hurt you, right?"

Shaking my head, I allowed my expression to answer her overly personal question.

"That's what I was worried about." Looking straight at me, capturing me in her stare, her eyes glazed over as she whispered, "You've been marked."

A gasp was all I could manage as her words kept repeating over and over in my head.

"Marked?" I repeated, unsure of myself. "Marked... by what?"

She studied my face, as if searching for the right answer to give. In an attempt to comfort me, she gently patted my hand and shook her head. "I do not know," she said, her voice no louder than a whisper. "And that worries me greatly."

THE HUNT

I left Granny's before the last batch had a chance to cool completely, the need to get home overwhelming me with each passing moment. Even though the truffles were small, they seemed to weigh a ton as I continued my trek through the darkened forest.

Gran wanted me to wait until morning, blubbering something about avoiding temptation in the night. But I knew my mother would flip her shit if I didn't make it back with these truffles. She had me on the schedule to set up for the festival this weekend, and the last thing I needed was her sending a search party out after me.

The old woman's worries were unfounded, and my trip back home was rather uneventful. In all honesty, I had hoped something would happen—something that would explain the odd feelings bubbling up inside me—something that would give me answers.

The darkness was rather quiet, my footsteps the only sound I could hear above my ragged breaths. I was thankful for my father's cloak as it kept me warm within the nighttime fall temperatures. The moon was nearly full, casting a blue glow over the otherwise colorful foliage.

The forest that frightened me mere hours before now made me feel content—at peace.

Breaking through the final line of trees, the world seemed much brighter as I stepped foot in the town's main square, my apartment only a few blocks away. The busy world suddenly came tumbling back to view, and I yearned for the quiet of nature and the woods from where I had just been.

I winced as a sudden burning sensation ripped through me, singeing my chest and tugging at my heart. It felt as if someone was grabbing me, making me ache to turn around and step foot back into the Shrouded Wood.

With the discomfort warring inside me, I pulled my cloak tighter around my neck and got down to one knee, begging for it to stop just long enough for me to think. Both confusion and temptation swirled around in my head, such a mixture of contradicting sensations. I felt as if I were being pulled by an unseen force—its long, powerful fingers gripping me, trying to pull me back into the forest.

I was about to bolt back into the protection of the tree line when the ache suddenly dissipated as I heard my name being called by an all-too-familiar voice.

"Rose!" Cody called out, dropping to his haunches in front of me and bowing his head to catch my eye. "Where have you been? I've been worried."

I was stunned for a moment, unsure of what just happened. The burning sensation was slowly ebbing away, like breath on glass. I took a moment to compose my breathing, trying to focus on my boyfriend, whose concerned face was mere inches from mine.

"Cody?" I mumbled, my vision clearing bit by bit. I took in his appearance, the light stubble on his young face, the bright, worried green eyes, and the small birthmark on his chin that took the shape of a purplish dot. Concentrating on his simple features helped me gain back my sense of composure.

"Rose?" Cody placed his hands on my shoulders to help steady me. "What's wrong?"

I shook my head, pushing off the ground and standing to my full height. He was a few inches taller than I was, but not enough to where I had to crane my neck to meet his eye, which I was thankful for at the moment. I was certain I would fall over if I had to tilt my head upward.

"I'm fine," I said, feeling like a broken record. I must have said that a hundred times today. Maybe if

I kept repeating it, like a mantra, it'd be true. "Just… felt dizzy for a minute."

Cody's frown didn't go unnoticed as he inspected my pale face. "Are you sure?" he asked, the skepticism never leaving his eyes. His gaze landed on the cut beautifying my forehead, and his concern increased. "What happened to your head?"

"Fell and hit a rock," I explained. "No big deal. My gran put some ointment on it to help it heal. Doesn't even hurt anymore."

"Okay, that's good," he said, seeming to accept my story and dropping the subject like a bad habit. Of course, that didn't stop him from prying about other things. "Where the hell have you been, by the way? I've been calling you for hours."

I sighed. "My mom made me go to my grandma's house to pick up some truffles for the festival this weekend," I said, lifting the basket full of chocolate goodness for him to see. "I'm sorry that I had to bail today."

He immediately eyed the basket with interest. "It's cool," he said, inching his hand toward the treats. "What took you so long then? You've been gone almost all day."

I slapped his hand away as he tried to sneak it into the basket. His pout was kinda cute, and a giggle escaped me before I could stop it.

"I was… sidetracked a bit," I answered, feeling good about not actually lying. Omitting some of the facts wasn't really lying… right?

"By what?"

"Don't worry about it," I said, using my granny's technique of waving my hand in his face to dismiss the subject. "Mind walking me to my mom's so I can drop these off?" I asked, holding up the basket.

Cody grinned. "No problem."

He took my free hand, and we began to walk away from the Shrouded Wood. Involuntarily, I glanced back at the line of trees bordering the path I had just emerged from moments before—the path that led back toward Granny's cottage.

Although I couldn't see anything, I felt as if something or someone was there… watching me… teasing me… tempting me to come back.

THE DODGE

We dropped off the truffles, my mom barely acknowledging us as she raced to prepare for the coming festival. There were only two days left until Halloween, and my mother apparently thought that meant it was the end of the world. Obviously, the only way to save it was to make sure everything on her list was checked off in triplicate.

Once I bid my mother a good night, I felt a little strange as Cody insisted we go back to his apartment. It wasn't that I had never stayed over with him. On the contrary, we weren't strangers to each other's beds. But tonight just felt, different, distant. I needed my space and had no real explanation or an idea of how to tell him this.

As soon as we walked in the door, the lock making me jump as it latched us in, Cody grabbed my wrist and yanked me to him, my body clashing harshly against his. Before I could protest, he brought his hand up to my face, feathering his fingers over the small cut along my hairline.

"Does it hurt?" he asked, concern etching new worry lines in his face. I just shook my head no, words lost on me at his sudden tenderness. It wasn't that Cody was always harsh, but we really didn't have much going on in this small town to really warrant different emotions like this. I think the last time he'd ever taken care of me was when I got a silly paper cut while working a summer job at the local bookstore—the *only* bookstore this tiny village had. Hell, a paper cut was the talk of the town.

As he looked into my eyes and scraped the pad of his thumb along my jaw, I could tell Cody wanted more than just simple company. He usually did. Most of the time, I was up for whatever—never really one to be picky when it came to even a little excitement in my life.

But tonight—tonight, I just wanted to sleep. It was as if my bed were calling me.

Calling…

Oh shit, calling!

"Crap!" I blurted just before his lips could make contact with mine.

"What?" he responded, backing away in alarm.

"I forgot to go get my phone. Jen is probably super pissed she hasn't heard from me all day." Jen—my roommate and partner in crime. We've known each other longer than we could say our own names, and I knew she would be livid with me for being MIA all day without taking my phone.

"She'll deal," Cody said, grabbing me by the waist and pulling me close again.

Pushing at his chest, I started to get annoyed with his overbearing behavior. "No, she won't. Not if I don't come home without a word."

With an overly dramatic sigh of exasperation, Cody ran his fingers through his hair before digging in his pocket and handing me his cell. "Here, call her and let her know you're staying with me."

Well, la-di-da. The man was just going to assume I would stay with him? Well, I had to admit, I did like his black satin sheets. They may have screamed *bachelor*, but they were still extremely comfortable—way more comfortable than my old, ratty, cotton sheets.

Dialing Jen's number, I took a deep breath, steeling myself for the shitstorm I was just about to drive into head-on.

She answered on the first ring. "Hey, Cody. I was just about to call you. Have you heard from our girl?"

"It's me, Jen."

"Holy fuck, woman! Do you realize how many times I called your phone before I realized it was sitting on your bed? And where the hell have you been?"

"Slow your roll, Jen. I was just at Granny's for the day." I could try to pacify her until I was blue in the face, and she'd still give me hell. It was one of the many things I adored about her.

"Don't tell me to slow my roll when you didn't even leave a note," she scolded. "Especially when you're going out into that creepy-ass forest by yourself."

"Hey, Jen?"

"What?"

"Get up from your throne and go look on the fridge," I instructed, grinning like a fool at what I knew would happen next. I was having fun picking on Jen, so when Cody started to get impatient, I ignored his exasperated looks.

"Why the hell do I need to look at the fridge? I know what a goddamn fridge looks like, Rose. And don't try to chang—" She stopped dead in her tracks before finally breathing out and saying, "Ohhhhh." Yeah, she saw my note.

"You're welcome," I said with a snotty lilt to my voice. "I'll accept your apologies over lunch tomorrow."

"Fine, but next time, I go with you," she demanded. "You don't need to be frolicking through those woods on your own."

"And what good would it do with you being there? You gonna protect me from the big bad wolf?" I joked, but the humor didn't seem to lighten my mood quite like it usually did. "I love you, Jen. I'll see you at BJ's Café tomorrow."

"Love you too, RoRo," she said, hanging up before I could holler at her for the stupid nickname.

Setting Cody's phone on the counter, I nearly leapt from my skin when a pair of strong arms enveloped me from behind. It didn't take but a moment to realize it was just Cody, his hard-on standing at attention and ready to go, even without me having to touch him.

"Why don't we take this huge thing off you and get comfortable... maybe in bed?" he said, nipping at my ear with his teeth and caressing my neck with his lips.

Pulling at the string on the front of my cloak, I allowed the heavy, red fabric to fall off my shoulders. Cody pushing it off me entirely and letting it pool to the floor had me pulling from his grip so I could bend over and pick it up. My dad's cloak never belonged on the floor.

Dutifully, I walked it over to the rack by the door and hung it up, wishing desperately I could just keep it on. For some reason, the cloak gave me comfort, as if my dad's arms were still wrapped in it, enveloping me, protecting me.

Cody's warm hand landed on my shoulder, snaking down the front of my chest to continue undressing me some more.

Then it hit me—the scratches over my heart began to sting—burn as if I had betrayed them somehow. It took all the strength I could muster not to cry out or show any discomfort as I pulled away from his touch.

Plastering a fake, apologetic smile on my face, I steadied my hands on his forearms and said, "Think we could just relax for tonight, lover boy? I'm so damn tired from walking all the way to and from Granny's house today. I could really use the rest."

Immediately, the pain in my chest eased—an inaudible sigh of relief leaving my lungs at the sudden feel of contentment.

Cody stared at me as if I had three heads. "Huh," he pondered. "I don't think you've ever turned me down before."

Blushing, I knew he was right. I wasn't usually the one to say no. "Well, today has kinda been a tough day for me. Do you mind if I take a rain check?" I put on my best puppy dog face as I tried to get him to reason with me. The last thing I wanted to do was explain these scratches on my chest.

"Sure," he said, shrugging and walking toward his room, adjusting his pants along the way. He didn't look too happy, but I would just have to worry about that later. For now, I needed some shuteye.

THE CALLING

"Rosetta..."

Extending my arm out, I felt around for Cody, my search coming up empty. I couldn't seem to find him. Didn't he just call my name? Sitting up, I blinked a few times and tried to adjust my sight. It didn't take me long to figure out that I was no longer in Kansas anymore, Toto. As a matter of fact, I didn't know where the hell I was. There was this strange haze surrounding me, both figuratively and literally.

Glancing around, I saw nothing but a dense fog, reminding me of early mornings in the Shrouded Wood. Yet, it couldn't have been the forest, because I was lying on something soft, comfortable.

Curiously, I inspected my surroundings. I could feel Cody's creamy, satin sheets beneath my fingers and scissored between my legs. The silken material felt great against my bare skin, deliciously over-sensitizing me. Wait, bare? I didn't want Cody seeing my wound!

Gasping, I pulled down the sheets to find that I was stark naked, my pale skin a contrast to the bright red of the bed. Red? Cody's sheets were usually that masculine black. Even though I was well aware I was no longer in his bed, I didn't feel frightened. The red color of the sheets seemed to make me feel amazingly sensual. Not only that, but the wound on my chest started tingling, igniting a whole new sensation of feelings inside me.

"Rosetta..."

I flinched, quickly covering myself up as I whipped my head around, trying to find the source of the voice. My wound began to burn, not uncomfortably so, but just enough to make me well aware it was still there. My desire became a tangible feeling, as if I could reach out and touch it at the very sound of this voice. Listening to someone call my name startled me a bit, but I wasn't scared. To my surprise, I was... content.

"Why are you hiding from me?"

A chill went down my spine at the... seductiveness *of the voice. Smooth, tantalizing, and... feminine.*

It was a woman who was calling out to me.

"Who... who's there?"

"Maybe you shouldn't be asking who *I am…" I froze as I felt hands wrap around my bare shoulders, fingers dancing over my skin, sending shivers all throughout my body—and to my wound. "…but* rather *what I am?"*

Her breath wafted over the back of my neck, igniting little fires along my skin. I could feel the surface beneath me shift as she moved closer to me, pressing her body against mine. I could feel her breasts against my shoulder blades, her nipples as hard as diamonds. The fact I enjoyed these feelings surprised me, especially since I'd never even considered a woman in a sexual manner before. My heart picked up pace in my chest, sending a whole new thrill to the core of my beautiful scratches.

Her hands traveled down my biceps at a measured pace, lips landing on the side of my neck. I took a shaky breath, turning my head to see who was teasing me. Suddenly, her hands were gone from my arms, gripping my head, and forcing me to keep my sight away from her.

"Not yet," she tutted, her voice breathy and low against my right ear. "Patience, my love. Patience…"

Normally, I would've been stubborn and insisted she let me peek, but I was utterly content to let her call the shots. She was in charge, and I loved every second of it.

As she leaned down to kiss behind my ear, I couldn't stop the moan that escaped me. Her hands slid back down to the soft skin of my shoulders, drawing circles with her thumbs to soothe me. I closed my eyes, relishing the warmth that spread through me at this mysterious woman's touch. She lit a fire in me that must've been lying dormant for so long.

"Am I dreaming?" I whispered breathlessly, feeling her left hand traveling down to my hip, her nails dragging along my side, making me tremble with need.

"Yes." I could feel her grin against the back of my neck. "But not for long, I promise. We're connected now. You'll seek me out, and we'll be together… forever."

Her hand slid lower, tantalizingly gliding its way between my legs. Even though I'd been touched there before, never had it felt this damn good. My heart quickened, my breaths becoming ragged as anticipation coursed through me, the wound on my chest throbbing with delicious torment. I bit my lip, fighting the urge to plea with her to enter me.

"It's time to wake up, Rosetta," she whispered. "Wake up."

Just as my body shivered with my climax, I opened my eyes to the real world.

THE CHANGE

I spent several minutes lying in Cody's bed in a daze. It was still early in the morning, much earlier than I usually woke up. Cody was snoring peacefully next to me, having rolled away at some point in the night—which was perfectly fine with me. I didn't think I could handle being in his arms at the moment. My body was still a knot of sensitivity from the dream, the skin around the areas where she touched me tingling, my muscles trembling. Warmth spread over my insides whenever I closed my eyes, remembering her soft caress and the feel of her lips against my neck. I occasionally had to stop myself before losing it.

Never had I experienced such a detailed, realistic dream like that, especially involving a woman. There was something about the dream, as if it were a vision—a premonition of my future rather than a hidden desire.

I couldn't handle being here in his bed any longer, the need to be alone overwhelming me with each passing moment. The dream felt so real, so powerful, it was as if having him around to witness it, even subconsciously, was like an invasion of my privacy.

Finally finding the energy to peel myself from under the sheets, I made it a point to move slowly so as not to wake him. The last thing I needed right now was a barrage of questions.

Still clothed, I managed to stay silent as I toed my shoes on, grabbed my cloak, and slunk out the door, placing my hood gently on my head as I made my way down the sidewalk. The sun was just waking up, and I couldn't remember the last time I'd been up this early. This tiny town was really rather beautiful in first light.

Sluggishly walking the few blocks to my apartment, I made it a point to examine the trees outlining the Shrouded Wood. What had happened to me out there? I knew I needed to learn more, yet the sudden adrenaline rush coursing through me at just the thought of stepping foot in the forest told me now was not the time.

Hurriedly, I picked up my pace and locked myself in my apartment, deciding on a shower to try and calm myself. I wasn't sure what was wrong with me, but ever since I blacked out the day before, I couldn't help but notice how strange I felt...

Turning on the bathroom light, I inspected myself in the mirror, assuming I'd find the reflection of some sallow-skinned girl with bed hair and a welt on her forehead. Instead though, I was shocked to find the person looking back at me did not resemble the girl I was just yesterday.

My skin was radiant, almost glowing. My hair was a little mussed up, which was to be expected, but it also had a sort of silken quality that hadn't been there before. I smoothed it back, letting my fingers tangle in the soft locks of my dark-colored hair, watching in the mirror as it flowed around my bare shoulders. Wispy, ethereal, I was having the best hair day imaginable.

Surprisingly, my mood matched my looks—both radiant and confused as hell.

As I examined myself in the mirror, I noticed something else about me that seemed out of place.

The welt that should have been a beacon on my forehead was no longer there.

Brushing a few stray strands of hair aside, I inspected the smooth skin of my forehead, finding no trace of a cut, bruise, or even a speck of dirt. I traced my index finger over the area where the wound had been the day before, feeling nothing but skin. There wasn't even any tenderness.

Damn, Gran's ointment really does work, was my first thought. I had worried that the gel would've rubbed off or something the night before, but apparently, my concern was rather unnecessary. It almost seemed… magical.

Lowering my gaze, I spied the three scratches over my heart. I was shocked to find that they too had healed. What should have been three giant, red lines of puffed skin were now thin marks that appeared to have already scarred over. Looking at them, you'd think I had gotten them years ago rather than just the day before.

I touched the new scars, feeling a tenderness that didn't come from pain…

"Rose?"

Jen knocked on the bathroom door, making me jump and nearly slip. I quickly caught myself, my heart hammering against my ribcage as she knocked again.

"I'm about to take a shower," I called out to her, turning to run the water to prove my point. "I'll be out in a few minutes."

She ceased her knocking, but I could hear her lean against the door, exhaling a slow breath.

"Glad you're home, but surprised to see you up and about this early. Want some coffee?"

I took a moment to contemplate her offer, thinking I might want to lie down after this. But no, we had too much to catch up on, and I still wasn't sure how much I wanted to tell my best friend.

"Sure," I responded louder than necessary. "I'll be out in a few."

I could practically feel her curiosity at my behavior through the door. "Okay," she said, pulling away so her voice was no longer muffled against the wood. "I'll make some breakfast too."

I sighed in relief, taking one last glance at myself—and the scars—in the mirror before stepping into the shower.

The warm water cascading over my skin never felt so good, my body obviously hyper-aware of every little sensation. Placing my face beneath the stream, I closed my eyes and immediately thought of her.

Who was she, and how the hell did she make me feel this good all from just one seemingly random dream? If I had to bet my life on it, I would've sworn her hands were really on me. After all, the sensations, not to mention that orgasm in the end, were all too real. My body still quaked at the thought.

Desperate for some answers, I touched the now-healed scars on my chest, digging my nails into the raised skin, hoping for some sort of sensation. The response I got shocked me to my core.

Desire, full-fledged craving, shot straight through me, and I suddenly ached for release.

Still clutching my hand over my heart, I slid the other down my body to cup my sex. It was as if I were allowing someone else to make the moves for me, imagining the woman from my dream coaxing me along, guiding me, and encouraging me.

Oh, the sensations I was feeling were completely foreign and new to me. Never had my body felt this sensitive—this good. Warmth sizzled through my insides, pooling in my gut, and making me wish I had her here to share my heightened desires.

I'd only dreamed of the woman once, and she was already getting to me in the most delicious of ways. Just as I began to wonder what it would feel like to have her mouth on me, my insides quickened, my climax coming at me from all sides. It was all the control I could muster not to scream with the barrage of sensations overtaking my body.

A sudden knock on the door had me jumping out of my skin, my body still high as a kite as it continued to come down from my release.

"Rose?" Jen called out through the door. "Are you okay? You've been in there for about an hour now."

An hour? Shit, it seemed like only five minutes had passed. Looking down at my fingers, I examined the odd wrinkles in my skin, evidence I had been beneath the water much longer than I thought.

"Uh, yeah. I'm fine," I hollered, clearing my throat to sound more human than I felt. "I'll be out in a sec."

"'Kay. Your omelet is getting cold."

"Shit," I cursed under my breath. What the hell was I going to say to Jen? Did I dare tell her what was happening to me? Hell, I didn't even know what was going on, so telling someone else would only make me sound like a nutcase.

For now, I would go through these changes alone—at least until I had some answers.

THE TIME

I was thankful that the cut on my forehead was gone, because I didn't want to deal with Jen losing her mind over me, being the klutzy fool that I was, getting hurt while out in the forest alone. She would often joke that the Shrouded Wood was possessed by monsters and evil spirits, and I didn't really feel like hearing about it when my head was still spinning with all of these peculiar emotions that had been plaguing me.

We ate breakfast with only light conversation to pass the time, Jen gushing about how excited she was for the Halloween festival and how cool she thought it was that my mom was the one putting it all together. I merely nodded and laughed when prompted. I felt a million miles away, but I did my best not to ignore my friend as she rambled on.

Following our one-sided conversation, Jen and I promised to meet at the coffee shop for lunch after she helped her sister prepare her booth at the festival. People all over the town had a specific job to do during the event—all assigned by my mother—and Jen's sister, Georgina, was in charge of the candy dispenser for the children. Since Georgina was manning that fiasco, it meant Jen would do most of the work, since her sister was a little on the lazy side and would most likely fudge the entire thing up.

Jen's words, not mine.

While she was away, I cleaned my room and vacuumed the apartment. I wasn't sure if I was feeling productive today or if it was all nerves, but I couldn't handle just sitting around. I felt the need to be in movement and figured cleaning up our pigsty was the best way to relieve some of the tension I had building up.

The entire time I was cleaning, all I could think about was the mystery woman from my dream. I could hear her voice in my head as if spoken directly in my ear. *Rosetta*—the memory of her continuing to repeat my name like a mantra haunted me. Her voice so smooth and seductive... it made me quiver with desire, even while still on my feet doing humdrum housework.

I tried to place the voice with one of the women in town. I had read somewhere that you could only dream about people you'd met in the real world, even if only for a second. That meant the voice had to belong to someone I'd met before. But, try as I may, I couldn't put a face to the tantalizing voice from my dream.

I gave a sigh as I finished putting away the vacuum cleaner, stuffing it in the closet with a huff. I was spending too much time fixating on a strange dream, trying to find meaning behind the images my subconscious mind conjured up.

"It was just a dream," I scolded myself. "It was probably just a random sex dream…" *About a woman,* my snide subconscious pointed out.

I tried to convince myself of this, but whenever my hand caressed the scars on my chest, a voice in the back of my mind told me there was more to the dream than I could possibly understand.

THE WALK

After there wasn't an inch of dirt left in the apartment, I threw on my red cloak and decided to go for a walk through town to help ease my mind. I was still bustling with energy, and I figured a nice, calm walk would be good for me, especially in this beautiful, fall weather.

I exchanged pleasant smiles with some of the other people in town, giggled at the young children shouting in excitement for the upcoming holiday, and watched what was left of the bird population begin their southern migration in the sky. It was such a pleasant day, and I found a peacefulness nestle within me from being out in the open air that I wasn't able to obtain from being inside.

As soon as Cody was awake and noticed my absence, he started texting me. After a few depreciating lines about waking up to find me gone, he asked if we could spend the afternoon together. With a guilty frown, I ignored his texts. As much as I needed a distraction, I felt that being around Cody wouldn't help me. The memory of how the scratches on my chest burned so painfully when he was close made me hesitant to even see him at the moment. I knew I was being silly, but with all the odd stuff going on, I felt the out-of-character act of ignoring my boyfriend was justifiable.

I found myself settling down by the lake that resided just within the town's limits and gazing out at the wrinkles in the water caused by the wind, the midday sun sparkling off the ripples like a sea full of diamonds. I lost myself in the sheer *calm* of the lake's atmosphere, my mind temporarily free of all doubt and worry. A light smile found itself on my lips, my eyes closing as I inhaled the fresh breeze that kissed my cheeks. I could have fallen asleep right then and there if I wanted to, but just as I was leaning back to lie down in the grass, I heard it.

Rosetta.

I opened my eyes and straightened immediately. It was *her* voice. The woman from my dream. I scanned the area, somehow praying that she'd be there. I knew the thought was silly though. How could she be here, in the real world? She was just a figment of my imagination... right?

Just as I was about to call out, my cell phone buzzed in my pocket, startling me. I nearly jumped out of my cloak when I felt it vibrate against my thigh.

Reaching into my pocket, I entertained the thought that maybe my dream woman was calling me, but, unsurprisingly, it was not. Jen's name shined on my phone's screen in bold lettering.

"Hey, Jen," I answered. "What's up?"

"Hey." Her voice came from the other end of the line. "I just got done collecting all the candy in town for Georgina. You ready for lunch?"

I nearly cursed aloud. With all of my daydreaming, I had overlooked the time and didn't realize it was lunchtime.

"Yeah," I said, brushing some hair from my face. "Just give me a few minutes. Totally zoned out by the lake."

"Oh! I love the lake," she chirped. "Stay right there. I'll pick up our lunch and meet you."

I smiled, glad that she wanted to have our lunch here. I was enjoying the peacefulness of the lake, and didn't want to have to leave it for the loud clutter of the coffee shop.

"Don't keep me waiting," I teased. "I'm hungry."

"I'm on my way," she said before hanging up.

It definitely didn't take the woman long to saddle up next to me with two delicious deli sandwiches and bottles of water. I was ravenous as I tore through the turkey on rye, my ladylike eating habits earning me a few sideways glances from Miss Prim and Proper.

"What?" I mumbled with a mouthful of sandwich nearly trickling from my lips. Catching a crumb that fell to the corner of my mouth, I used my middle finger to scoop it up and licked it off.

"Nothing," she said, shaking her head as if she thought I'd lost my marbles. "I've just never seen you eat so... quickly. Lucky you're not inhaling the napkin too."

"Heh. I'd never do that." Though, if any more of the sandwich fell on the wrapper in my lap, I might've had to make an exception.

"What's up with you, anyway? You're not pregnant, are you?"

Of course, she'd say that just as I was taking a rather large gulp of water. At the sound of the P-word, I couldn't help but spew clear liquid all over the grass in front of me.

"You did not just ask me that," I said in disbelief, wiping at the dribble on my chin.

"Well? You've been staying at Cody's quite a bit lately, and you're eating like a pig on steroids." She shrugged. "It's a valid assumption. Thank cripes you're not hurling all over the place though."

"Jen, I'm not pregnant," I said with an adamant shake to my head.

"Then what's up with you?"

Just as she asked, my phone, which was sitting between us in the grass, began to vibrate with a new call. Seeing Cody's name on the screen, I quickly swiped to ignore it. No one needed to know I had been dodging his calls all morning. He probably wanted to know why I had bailed on him before he woke up.

"Uh huh," she said in a singsong voice before taking another bite of her sandwich. Speaking with her mouth full, she added, "I'm guessing someone didn't get any last night."

I shrugged. "I just didn't feel like it."

"Things going okay between you two?"

I could tell her question was not meant to be nosey, but more out of concern than anything else. Could I tell her about how I'd been feeling the past twenty-four hours? I mean, did I even know enough to tell her? Surely not. At the moment, I just needed to sit back and let things pass—either that, or figure out what the hell was wrong with me before I started burdening Jen with my issues… or non-issues. Who the hell knew at this point?

"Things are fine. Just been busy helping my mom is all." It was partially true, the helping part anyway. Though it seemed like I'd spent most of the day yesterday repeating the words *I'm fine* over and over again. I was actually beginning to believe them—for a second.

Jen seemed skeptical at first, but she didn't push it. She could tell there was something bothering me—best friend's intuition, I suppose—but knew not to pry if I didn't willingly share on my own. I felt a little guilty keeping things from her, but this was something for me to deal with—at least until I could figure out what the heck it really was I was dealing with.

We sat and enjoyed the beautiful scenic lake view for a while longer, finishing our lunch and exchanging stories of our day's events. Her day was much more exciting than mine, as she detailed her sister's blushing face when they ran into a guy she liked while out shopping for candy. When I told her I had cleaned up the apartment, she laughed and hugged me in gratitude.

It was a nice distraction.

THE VISIT

When it came time for us to part—Jen wanting to go meet up with her group of friends and I opting to check in on my mom rather than join her—we said our goodbyes and headed off in different directions. I usually enjoyed gathering with all of the girls, trading harmless gossip and having a group consensus that nothing interesting ever happened in town, but I felt that being in a large group would only agitate me, so I decided that a trip to my mom's would be a good idea.

On the way there, I had to ignore two more calls from Cody. Why couldn't he just take the hint and leave me alone? If I wasn't answering, there was obviously a reason. As bad as I was feeling for ignoring my boyfriend, he was starting to really annoy me.

Pulling my cloak closer around my body, I gave my mom's door three knocks before letting myself in. She and I were never private from each other, so it wasn't an odd occurrence for me to just barge into my old house unannounced. I only knocked to give her a few seconds to stash the bodies… or maybe make herself decent on a normal day.

"Mom?" I called out.

"In the living room, Rosie!"

I nearly rolled my eyes at my mother's baby name for me. Ever since I was little, she called me Rosie, and even though I was a full-grown woman, she still insisted on it. I was pretty certain she only did it because she knew it bugged me.

"When are you going to stop calling me that?" I teased as I found her sitting on the couch, looking over some papers. No doubt double-checking the schedule for the festivities, booth locations, and the like. The woman never stopped working, I swear.

"When I'm dead," she replied cheekily. "To what do I owe the visit?"

"What?" I said, sitting on the couch next to her. "I can't come visit my favorite mommy?"

"Your *only* mommy, as far as you know." She shot me a grin. "I forgot to thank you for picking up the truffles last night. I've been so swamped with all of this preparation that I'm losing my mind."

"Can't lose something you don't have, Mom," I said. "And don't worry about it. I love visiting Granny."

"How was the trip?" she asked. "Everything go okay?"

I paused to think about everything that had been happening since the day before. Did Granny somehow tell her something? I had to contemplate whether this was a trick question or if I should just blow it off as my mom's normal way of making small talk.

"Yup," I said, making the P sound pop with my dry lips. "Nothing to speak of."

"That's good." She paused, a curious look crossing her face. Uh oh, what did she hear? "So, have your costume all ready to go for tomorrow?"

Breathing a sigh of relief, I smiled and was more than thankful to tell her about my attire. "Yes, actually. I found this adorable red dress that matches Daddy's cloak perfectly," I explained as I palmed the soft fabric wrapped around me. "It has a corset built in to the bodice with a short, lacy skirt. I also bought some fishnet stockings and red heels."

"That sounds cute!" she exclaimed, excited to hear that I was actually dressing up. Just a few days ago, I told her only children dress for Halloween and I'd feel silly in a costume. But this one was tailored to my liking, and I wasn't bound to represent any specific character. I could just be… me.

"I also found a gorgeous gold mask with ruby inlays. It'll be the perfect addition to the outfit." I beamed.

"That sounds just perfect for you, Rose," she said, smiling sincerely before putting her nose back into her paperwork.

We sat in silence for a few moments, and suddenly, things seemed awkward between us. Could've just been me, but the fact that I didn't feel confortable sitting in silence with my own mother strengthened my awareness that something was up with me. I had to do something to get my mind off last night's dream.

"Hey, Mom. Need any help with anything? You know, before tomorrow?" I asked, hoping she'd say yes so I didn't go stark mad in my own skin.

"Actually… yes," she answered, her expression brightening at the thought. "Tabetha was supposed to help me set up the pumpkins around the town square and hang the lanterns between buildings, but she bailed, saying something about her back hurting. Girl just didn't want to do the work from what I can tell because I saw her riding her horse about an hour after she told me. I was just about to go do it myself, but I could really use the help. We'd probably get it done twice as fast together. You up for it?"

"Definitely," I said, clapping my hands together once and jumping up from the chair. "I'll go load up the pumpkins."

THE CRY

Dragging my red-hooded ass into my apartment was a feat after the exhausting work my mom had me doing all night. Not only did that woman want me to help her hang lanterns and put out pumpkins, but I had to carve the damn things too. I was so not aware of just how much help she needed and was lucky I'd managed to get it all done before two in the morning.

Staying as quiet as possible so as not to wake Jen, I tiptoed into my room and lit a candle, feeling the need for muted light at such a late hour. I contemplated a bath, but was just too damn exhausted to even think of doing anything other than planting my face in my pillow.

Tossing my phone on my desk, I noticed the obscene amount of missed calls and text messages that littered my notifications. Rolling my eyes, I shut the damn thing off and pushed it out of my mind. I was way too tired to worry about the boy's feelings right now.

With the cool weather rolling in, I opened my window just a crack so I could feel the glorious chill fill my room, cooling my body that had been worked to the bone all evening. Stripping down to nothing, I was able to see my scars again for the first time since that morning.

The urge to touch them, caress them, protect them, seemed to overwhelm me as I stood by my window with my hand over my heart. My breathing quickened at just the feeling of power and desire it gave me.

Did it really *give* me those feelings? Or was someone, or something, behind these passions that seemed to overwhelm me? Granny's words repeated in my head like a broken record... *you've been marked.*

But by what? And for what purpose?

Well, something could mark me all it wanted, but there wasn't much I could do about it if I didn't know what it meant... right?

With the blood pumping through my veins, I made it a point to breathe, feeling the throb of my heart through the scratches on my chest. Looking down, I could see their beauty—marveling at the sight of the patterns etched in my skin.

Suddenly, a pang of craving hit me like a wrecking ball, slamming me with such mixed emotions of lust, need, adoration... it took my breath away. At that very moment, a wolf howled in the distance, bringing my attention back to the open window where the nearly full moon lit the night sky.

The sound seemed so sad, so distant. Almost like the wolf was calling out to a long-lost mate, desperate for the day they'd finally be able to be together. Then again, it was probably my imagination getting the better of me—with it being All Hallows Eve, a nearly full moon, and almost three in the morning.

Looking at the clock again, I sighed in disbelief. I couldn't believe I'd been standing there naked in front of the open window for over a half hour. Anybody who was out walking on the street below would get an eye-full if they looked up. With that thought, my body slumped in pure exhaustion, and I sluggishly padded over to my bed.

It didn't take long for the sandman to come snatch me up in a whirlwind of dreams.

THE PROTECTOR

The sticks and leaves against the bare pads of my feet didn't seem to hurt as I ran through the Shrouded Wood. Running... from something... though I wasn't sure what. My heart pounded and my scars burned as I sprinted through the thick trees—terror streaking through me.

I was bare beneath my cloak, naked, except for the golden, ruby-encrusted mask on my face. My legs felt like they were getting heavier, weighted down by an unknown force, causing me to slow. Frantic, I fell against the forest floor, padded by leaves of all colors, my cloak covering my body like a shimmering waterfall of blood. I scrambled forward, unsure of what was following me, but needing to get away—far, far away.

Suddenly, I saw it. Or, rather... them. Three sets of eyes, glowing blue in the moonlight, stalking toward me like I was some kind of prey they had been hunting for miles. I was frozen, paralyzed by fear. I knew damn well if I stood and tried to run, they would catch me. I was certain of it. The hunger in their eyes spoke volumes.

I was done for.

Suddenly, the first one, spittle dripping from the fangs that poked through its rubbery lips, lunged, barreling toward me at lightning speed, the other two following close behind it. Before I could yell out, scream for someone to save me, a large ball of fur leapt over my prone body, coming face-to-face with my attackers.

She was magnificent. From the sandy color of her fur, to her strong, powerful stance... everything about her radiated protector, *not* attacker. *The others regarded her with eyes that spoke of betrayal and fury, their snarls fierce and dangerous. As I watched her lunge for them, I suddenly felt heavy-hearted that I had caused this. Because of me, she had to fight her own kind. Why she felt the need to protect me was beyond my comprehension as my head began to lull to the side. I couldn't seem to keep my eyes open, though I wanted to make sure she was okay.*

Without another moment's notice, my arms buckled and my upper body crashed to the forest floor as everything around me went black.

THE EYES

"Rosetta..."

Arms. Strong, feminine arms enveloped me, held me, as my eyes began to flutter open. Moaning, I examined my surroundings, unsure of exactly where I was. I could tell I was still in the Shrouded Wood, but not in the same place where I had passed out moments before.

"Rosetta..."

The feel of my name caressing my ear, the breath warm and inviting, had me tilting my head back, inviting more of the tantalizing feel against my skin. Soft, gentle lips caressed the length of my neck, sprinkling my skin with chills and making me whimper with need.

"There you are, my love," she crooned, still poised behind me so I couldn't see her.

"Mmm... you're back," I mumbled, unable to fully speak at the moment, but needing to let her know I knew she was the same woman from the night before.

"I'm always here, my sweet Rosetta."

Bringing my arm up, I reached behind me to feel her, my hand landing on a soft, warm cheek—long strands of hair brushing against my knuckles.

Fingernails trailed down my arm, starting where I touched her and gliding all the way until she reached the side of my torso, lightly brushing the very edge of my breast. Looking down, I watched her beautiful hand as it came around and trailed back up the center of my chest.

Claws. Sprouting from her fingertips were real, actual claws. While I should've been scared, I wasn't. The claws were unmistakable, yet beautiful, the perfect size and shape for her. It wasn't until she reached the scars on my chest that I realized... they matched up flawlessly.

"You..." I whispered, my lips quivering at the thought.

"Yes," she hissed, her lips precariously close to my ear. "Do I frighten you, my lovely Rose?"

"No," I said, not an ounce of doubt in my mind. "I was hoping it would be you."

A light whimper caressed my cheek, almost as if she had been waiting for me to say the words— accept her for who she was. Sharp teeth grazed the soft padding of my earlobe as her claws lightly dug the same pattern over my heart, never breaking the skin, but sending a whole new wave of longing through me.

Continuing her hold, she wrapped her other hand beneath my chest, cupping one of my breasts in her strong, lean hand. As her fingers caressed over my nipple, I inhaled a sharp intake of breath, relishing the feel of her touch against my skin.

"Do you like it when I touch you?" she asked as her clawed fingers grazed up the soft expanse of my neck and to my jaw, her thumb tracing little patterns over my lips.

Biting and then kissing the pad of her thumb, I sighed and said, "God, yes." My voice sounded strong, urgent, like my soul was thirsty and she was the only one who could quench it. Her grip tightened on my nipple as she toyed with my breast.

The fact I still had my mask on didn't seem to bother me any, but I wanted to see her without obstruction—see who this woman was who was haunting these delicious, wonderful dreams. So, in turn, I wanted her to be able to see me.

When I reached up to remove the golden mask, her hand left my breast and stopped me.

"No, love. Keep it on. It looks so beautiful against your striking, blue eyes," she said, soothing the act of denial with a kiss to my fingers.

"I want to see you," I said, my voice pleading for her to understand.

"And you will, in due time. For now, I want to satisfy you. Make you tremble in my arms," she whispered against my ear.

Grabbing my face in her hand, she turned me around, forcing me to face sideways. My eyes fluttered shut just as her lips landed on mine. Her grip loosened as her kiss deepened, causing me to arch my back and beg for more. Her lips were soft and plump with just a hint of strength to tell me just what she wanted.

I gladly opened to her, the potent feel of her tongue swimming with mine had my insides quickening. She met my demands just as much as I met hers—match for match—we were perfect together. Never had a first kiss felt this damn good.

Moaning, I linked my hands behind her neck, my vigor letting her know just what she did to me, how my body reacted to her touch. Oh, I didn't think I could get enough of this, yet wondered if my body could handle any more, all in the same thrust of her tongue.

She seemed to know just how to do me in.

Pulling away, I nearly whimpered at the loss of her lips until I heard her soothing voice.

"Keep your eyes closed, Rosetta. Right now, I just want you to sense me. Feel how I feel," she said against my lips. I nodded, the need to obey her like second nature to me. "Now, lie back and get comfortable," she instructed, easing me down against the plush forest floor, my cloak the only barrier between my naked body and the leaves.

As soon as I was completely relaxed, she left my side. I nearly opened my eyes to see where she had gone, but remembered her instructions and chose to obey.

"Good girl," she praised, her voice still mere inches from my head. As if in slow motion, I could feel her naked body press against my side. She was so soft, so warm, the stark opposite of a man. It amazed me just how much I was truly enjoying her attention and couldn't wait to return the favor. I only wished I knew whether we'd still be together for me to give her the attention she deserved in return.

"Shh," she shushed. "No more thinking right now, Rosetta. Just feel and enjoy."

The feel of her lips touching the scar over my heart nearly did me in. A loud gasp left my mouth as waves of pleasure rippled through me each time my heart picked up a beat, her lips a catalyst to my desire.

Slowly, methodically, she made her way down my body, touching each part of my soul with her mouth and making me writhe with need. She licked both of my nipples, making them hard until they were silently begging for more attention. The feel of her warm lips closing over each bud had me uncontrollably unsteady beneath her, unable to stay still as she paid close attention to my needs. I welcomed her silky, indulgent touch as she kissed the soft slope of my stomach, her chin grazing down the top of my pelvis to make me tremble. As soon as she reached my thighs, nibbling and kissing each one in a tantalizing rhythm, I cried out, desperately in need of her mouth on me.

"I need you to— Oh, I need—"

"Shh, Rosetta. I know just what you need, love," she whispered, *her breath sending tingles of pleasure straight to my sex. God, she was close. So close.*

Thrusting my hips up, I tried to show her what I needed from her—make it obvious I was painfully waiting for her mouth to make contact.

"Patience," she whispered, *and I could feel her breath against me, her mouth so tantalizingly close.*

As soon as her warm tongue came into contact with my clit, I cried out a mixture of unrecognizable words, the feeling exploding inside me like a cannonball. My back arched and my hips thrust forward, forcing her to steady me with her hands.

I was already so hyperaware of every little move she made, every little thing she did with that tormenting mouth, that I was definitely not going to last long. And she knew it too.

Picking up the pace, she began a back-and-forth motion with her lips, her tongue, her jaw—oh, it was just simply amazing. With one of my hands knotted in her hair, I laid the other on my chest, over my heart. Every sensation I felt down there echoed through my scars, the sensations both confusing and mind-blowing.

She was the sole reason I felt this way—the sole reason I wanted to stay here in this forest forever.

Her sucking on my clit sent jolts of pleasure through me, my insides tightening at a rapid pace, my heart nearly fluttering out of my chest. Streams of moans escaped me and echoed off the barren trees around us, my body losing all control at the hands of this striking woman.

Climbing higher, I could feel the prickles of sensation all the way to my feet as my core trembled and shuddered beneath her lips. Crying out, I plummeted off the edge in a free-fall of pure ecstasy. As I started coming back down from this breathtaking climactic high, she pulled away and called my name.

"Rosetta, look at me. I want to see your eyes," she instructed.

Panting, I tried to catch my breath as I tilted my head up in her direction. Opening my hooded gaze, I looked beyond the mask to the woman who had just given me the most intense orgasm of my life.

Piercing, golden eyes stared back at me. She simply took my breath away.

THE TEARS

Waking up, I quickly bolted upright, grabbing my head when a dizzy spell overtook my senses. I was still out of breath, my body sweaty and tingly, as if I was still trembling from that amazing post-climactic haze.

No way all that had been just a dream. She seemed so real.

Looking out the window, I saw the day had started long ago and my eyes immediately darted toward my clock. It was already well after noon. The thought that I had a few hours before the festival began made me sigh in relief.

Panting, I touched the scar on my chest and immediately felt a pang of sadness. What if I was just going crazy? What if all these dreams meant nothing and she didn't really exist?

Without warning, a tear emerged and pooled in the corner of my eye. For the first time in quite a while, I felt like crying. Crying for the loss of someone that seemed so real in my dreams yet didn't exist in real life was just silly. Well, in theory. But in my heart, it made me sad to think that I would only have her in my dreams.

Internal judgments be damned, I couldn't help but lay my head back down on my pillow and sob. I so badly needed for her to be real. My life seemed so boring before, but now it felt even emptier, like I was a shell of a woman. I had nothing that truly fulfilled me—nothing that really made me happy.

Until her.

I lay there for some time, venting my anguish into my pillow. I felt so small in that moment, so insignificant. The closest thing I'd ever had to true love existed solely in my dreams, and the mere thought of that made me want to curl under my blankets until she returned to me.

A few minutes passed as I cried before I heard a tentative knock come from the other side of my door.

"Rose?" It was Jen, sounding worried. I must have been sobbing louder than I thought I was.

I quickly wiped my eyes clean of the tears the best I could and cleared the giant lump from my throat before answering, "Y-Yeah?"

"Are you okay?" she asked softly, not daring to enter the room without my permission, to which I was eternally grateful.

"Yes, I'm fine," I said, my new apparent catchphrase spilling from my lips again, while I wished with everything I had that it were true.

"Right…" She sounded disbelieving. She was silent for a moment, making me fear that she was going to pry. I didn't think I could handle that right now. I was already a mess—one sympathetic look away from drowning in sorrow. Finally, after what felt like an eternity of waiting, she said, "Are you almost ready? The festival starts soon."

I sighed in relief, once again trying to clear my eyes of the leftover tears. I had a better grasp on my emotions now that Jen had come along to focus me. I felt a little childish having broken down like that, but whenever the thought crossed my mind that I'd possibly never see the woman of my dreams in the waking world, I felt a hitch in my breath.

"I just need to shower," I replied, peeling myself from the plush surface of my bed, now soaked in sweat and tears. "Once I'm dressed, I'll meet you there, okay?"

Jen took a moment to respond. "Okay, if you say so," she said. She lapsed into another bout of silence before saying very gently, "Are you sure you're okay, RoRo?"

Her concern warmed my heart, even through the use of that horrid nickname. With everything going on, it was nice to know I had such a wonderful best friend.

"Don't worry about me," I said to her. I couldn't say I was fine anymore, because that was a lie. I was *not* fine. I was far from it, to be honest. I was possibly going crazy with dreams about wolves and an alluring woman with claws. That didn't classify as *fine* in my book.

"I always worry," she said softly, tenderly, her voice muffled by the wooden barrier between us. "You're my friend, Rosetta. I'll always worry about you."

I smiled, though she couldn't see it. "Thank you, Jen."

"No need," she said, then switched her tone to a more jovial one for my benefit. "Now hurry up! It's Halloween, and there's candy and boys to be devoured!"

I laughed, shaking my head as I collected my dress from the closet and set it out on my bed. "I'll be right behind you, promise."

"See ya there."

I listened as Jen walked away, the front door closing behind her after she exited our apartment. I let my smile remain on my lips for a few seconds before an all-too-familiar voice whispered in the back of my mind.

Rosetta...

"Please be real," I whispered to the voice. "Please... just please be real..."

THE MASK

After showering and primping myself up a little
bit—it was a special occasion, was it not?—I got
dressed in my costume and stood in front of my
body-length mirror to admire it.

The dress was a little tight, but that was just
what I wanted. The corset was a snug fit around my
waist and chest, showing off a generous amount of
cleavage, but not enough to give up my sense of
class... *I hope*. The red dress billowed around my
knees, the lace caressing the skin of my legs
whenever I moved. Combined with my daddy's red
cloak, I felt, for lack of a humbler term, beautiful.

The scratches on my chest tingled at the thought,
almost as if agreeing with me. Just a hint of raised
skin peeked above the fringe of the corset, and a
sneaky smile played on my lips at the thought of my
little secret. Only those who stared at my breasts
would notice, and the cloak would likely cover the
bit that was exposed anyway. A little part of me
wanted to show off my new beauty marks, yet the
part who didn't want to be bombarded with
questions shot that idea down quickly.

Once I stepped into my matching red heels, I stood by my open doorway, staring down at the golden mask lying on my dresser. The sight of it made me think of the woman—*again*. It made me recall the way she'd said it looked beautiful contrasted against my blue eyes, and how she stopped me from taking it off by kissing my fingers, sending delightful tingles through me from her tender touch. I sucked in a deep breath, closing my eyes and willing my heart to slow its erratic thumping within my chest at the delicious memory.

What did it say about me when this woman could excite me so without even being here?

Slowly, I placed the mask on my face and secured it so that it wouldn't fall off before making my way to the festival.

THE CLAIM

I got to the town square just on time, having only spent about an hour getting ready. There was still some time before things really picked up, so when I arrived, there were mostly just the booth handlers meandering about, as well as a sparse number of children running around excitedly in their cute superhero and princess costumes. A smile snuck its way onto my face as I watched them all mill about the open street.

I spotted Jen and her sister, Georgina, preparing the candy dispenser a little ways up the street. I hadn't been able to see it before, but Jen looked cute in her Esmeralda costume, her hair fluffed up with a pink ribbon to match that of the gypsy character from *The Hunchback of Notre Dame*. Georgina was equally as cute, although in a more childish way, with her Dorothy Gale costume, complete with frilly pigtails and wicker basket. I contemplated joining them, but they seemed rather preoccupied with preparing the dispenser and shooing away impatient children who wanted some candy.

I moved along, waving to those who ran the dunking booth, the Bobbing for Apples buckets, and the young men who were helping the local band set up the stage for some atmospheric music.

I had to admit… my mom knew how to throw a party.

The sky began to dim as time flew by, the faint outline of the coming full moon visible behind the clouds in the east. More and more people arrived to enjoy the festival, *oohing* and *ahhing* at all the booths and the carved pumpkins my mom and I had laid out throughout the street. I felt a swell of pride when a group of children stopped to marvel at a particular jack-o'-lantern with the face of a wolf carved into it. That one was my favorite by far.

I briefly wondered if my partialness towards the pumpkin with a wolf's face on it had inadvertently inspired my dream the night before. It wouldn't have been the first time my dreams were affected by my experiences in the waking world.

Melancholy threatening to sour the moment, I left the children to praise my pumpkin carving and continued to stroll the streets.

I was looking around for my mom, expecting her to be shouting orders at the people who volunteered to help set up the festival, when I bumped into someone by mistake. The crowd was beginning to thicken, and it was becoming more difficult to navigate through the throng of bodies, especially in high heels. I nearly fell over as my shoulder collided with someone larger than me, our bodies crashing together awkwardly like two drunkards.

"Ah, I'm sorry!" I yelped, stumbling a bit in order to right myself. Damned heels and their lack of balance. "I didn't see you there…"

"Rose?"

I looked up to find Cody staring back at me, half of his face covered by a black eye-patch. He was dressed as some sort of pirate, wearing a white lace-up shirt with ruffled cuffs and collar. He even pulled off the black knickers like a pro. On his feet were black boot tops, covering a pair of normal sneakers, and on his head was a tri-fold pirate hat with the skull and crossbones logo on it. He looked like a swashbuckler straight from the Renaissance with his eye-patch and toy sword attached to his hip.

"Oh…" I said, suddenly feeling incredibly awkward. "Hi, Cody."

"Where the fuck have you been?" he demanded, reaching up to pull off the eye-patch so I could see the frustration in both of his eyes. "I've been calling and texting since yesterday."

I cursed inwardly. I had left my phone back at the apartment, my dress having no pockets to carry it in. I had forgotten to check it before I left. It no doubt had twice as many missed calls and text messages than the night before when I turned it off.

"I'm sorry, Cody," I said gently. "I've been going through some stuff, and I needed to be alone for a while."

He scowled at me. "What could you possibly be going through that I can't help with?" His glower took on a more inquiring quality to it as he inspected me. "And what happened to the cut on your head? It's just... gone."

"Can we talk somewhere more private?" I pleaded quickly, feeling uncomfortable as people turned and stared at us. "I'd rather not have an audience."

Cody didn't say anything. He just nodded and allowed me to lead him away from the festival's crowd. I spotted Jen watching us from behind the candy dispenser, a worried frown on her face. I shook my head at her to let her know nothing was wrong. She didn't look very appeased when I lost sight of her.

The festival, thankfully, was taking place in the town's main square, which was not too far from the lake where Jen and I ate lunch the day before. I led him close to the embankment before turning to him with my arms crossed.

"Okay," I said with a sigh. "Go ahead."

"Why are you so cavalier about this?" he groaned. "You've been acting weird ever since you went to your grandma's house the other day. What's going on?"

"I've just got some stuff to sort out," I said. "I'm sorry that I ignored you... I really am. I just felt like being alone for a while, okay?"

"It's not okay," he said with some force. "I'm your boyfriend. You're supposed to come to me if you've got a problem so I can fix it."

A frown found its way onto my face. "So *you* can fix it?" I echoed. "You don't think I can handle myself?"

"No, that's not what I meant." He ran a hand over his eyes in exasperation. The gesture irritated me for some reason. "What I mean is... you should have come to me."

"I'm sorry," I said, trying to calm myself. "But, this isn't something you can help me with."

"What *is* it though?" he pushed. "What is so bad that you can't tell me of all people?"

"It's my business," I said, a little harsher than I meant to. Not wanting to start a scene, I sighed and lowered my voice. "I'll deal with it, okay? Now, if you'll excuse me…"

I tried to walk past him to go back to the festival, but his hand shot out and gripped my upper arm. I gasped as he whipped me around to face him, his expression set in a mask of anger.

"I want to know what's wrong with you," he growled in a low, demanding tone. "*Now.*"

I stared at Cody in shock, witnessing a side of him I had never seen before. He had always been cheery, sarcastic, and at times, a bit overbearing, but never had he been this scowling, violent man that he was now. The scars on my chest began to burn, but I ignored them for the moment, composing myself so I could speak as calmly to him as possible.

"Cody," I said, his name spilling from my lips slowly, placidly. "Let go of my arm."

"Not until you actually tell me what the *fuck* is up with you!" he barked, shaking me violently. "I'm tired of these games, Rosetta. Tell me why you've been ignoring me, right now!"

His tone of voice, the way he stared directly into my eyes, and how he dug his fingertips into my bicep almost painfully set me off. The burning that originated from the three scratches on my chest radiated throughout my entire body, spreading to my very toes like a wildfire of wrath. I could feel it coalescing in the center of my chest, forming into a raging inferno of pure, unadulterated *fury.*

I didn't feel fully aware of myself in that moment. The edges of my vision blurred, my form trembling, as I lunged at Cody, my sights set directly on him. His expression was that of surprise as I tore his hand away from my arm and brought my fist up, smashing it against the bridge of his nose. He roared out in pain as blood spurted from both of his nostrils, his nose bending awkwardly to the left. Flailing for a moment, he stumbled backwards as crimson continued to spill over his lips and down his chin until his feet tangled together and he fell over the edge of the embankment. He slammed headfirst to the ground, rolling until he was sprawled out just on the cusp of the waterline.

Almost immediately, I realized what I had done and yelled out to him. Racing down the slope to his side, I kneeled next to him to make sure he was all right. I pulled him onto his back, wincing as I saw the now-crooked shape of his nose and the blood that continued to ooze from his nostrils. To think *I* had done that… I was almost sick.

Cody was unconscious, I deduced, as he didn't respond to me calling his name. Frantically, I felt around his body, making sure nothing else was broken. I breathed a sigh of relief when I found nothing out of place.

"What the hell just happened to me?" I whispered to myself, frustration taking over me. I slammed my fist into the ground, growling in time with the loud thump. I had been overcome by my anger, had succumbed to the rage that flooded my system. Now Cody was unconscious with a severely broken nose, all because of me.

What was I to do?

A strange rumbling noise above caught my attention. I quickly turned, my eyes widening at what I saw.

Eyes, shining the color of gold, stared at me from the top of the embankment. My throat constricted at the sight of the wolf from my dream, standing proud over me with her sandy brown mane rustling in the breeze. She was even more magnificent in real life, with her regal stance and the elegant slope of her body. Her fur looked soft and clean, unlike the coarse mange they depicted wild wolves having. I was suddenly taken with the urge to walk up and run my fingers through her beautiful mane…

Her eyes darted quickly to the prone form of Cody, sniffing the air tentatively, as if seeking something. She met my gaze once again, then bowed her head and turned away.

"Wait!" I called, jumping to my feet, my unconscious boyfriend forgotten. "Don't go!"

The wolf glanced over her shoulder at me, something akin to playfulness glinting in her shimmering eyes. She gave a huff, and then bolted.

I didn't hesitate for even a second.

I gave chase.

The wolf was swift, agile. She loped along the street with elegance, avoiding the eye of the town's people with practiced ease. Except me. She always made sure to slow whenever I was starting to lose sight of her.

She was playing with me, I realized. She kept glancing back at me, her eyes shining with joy, almost as if to sing, "Come and get me!"

I pumped my legs as hard as I could. I had discarded my heels in favor of running on my bare feet, the sound of them slapping against the concrete like a hand to the face. I felt strangely wild, almost carefree. The wind whipped against my face, my hair and cloak blowing behind me like the cape of a superhero. I felt *invigorated*. As if I were enjoying this little game of cat and mouse.

The wolf gave a wide berth to the festival, which was a relief. I didn't think an oversized wolf running through a crowd would go over well with the partygoers. I watched with amazement as she zigzagged through the streets, the sun beginning its descent—kissing the horizon. Night was quickly approaching, the outline of the full moon starting to solidify high in the eastern sky. I quickened my pace with this thought, not wanting to lose her in the darkness of night.

For a while, I didn't know where the wolf was going, but then it dawned on me just as we turned a sharp corner and the light of the surrounding lanterns illuminated the tree line ahead.

The Shrouded Wood.

The wolf disappeared into the crowd of trees, and, for the first time since I started chasing her, I hesitated. Everything had started with the Shrouded Wood. The mysterious scratches, the dreams, the mood swings... all of it began while I was walking through the forest on my way to my granny's house.

"What do I do?" I wondered aloud, uncertain of myself.

As if in answer, I heard a howl resonate throughout the air, settling into my soul and spurring me on.

"That's that, then."

Dislodging one of the lanterns from its post near the tree line, I held it in front of me to illuminate the way as I pressed on into the Shrouded Wood.

I'd barely made it a few yards before the sun finished its descent and the full moon's light blanketed the forest in a sea of blue. I was glad for my forethought with bringing the lantern. Otherwise, I'd be trying to navigate the path with minimal illumination. Although, I was wishing I had kept the heels, because my bare feet were starting to sting from stepping over the dead leaves.

Holding the lantern over my head, I walked along the forest path in search of the wolf. She disappeared within the brush and had yet to reveal herself as I called out.

"Please, come back!" My voice echoed throughout the Shrouded Wood, bouncing off the trees and back at me, as if I were being mocked. "Please?"

A voice in the back of my mind pointed out that I had no clue what I would do once I actually caught the wolf. What could I possibly get out of this? A wolf couldn't tell me why I'd been having these feelings.

Or could it?

I felt like I had left my world and entered some sort of alternate dimension. Where wolves played games with you, attractive women haunted your dreams, and your boyfriend turned out to be a huge dick...

Oh shit!

I stopped walking as realization dawned on me. *Cody.* I'd just left him there! His nose was broken, and he might have a concussion from his fall. I cursed aloud at my own stupidity. I'd been so enamored with catching the wolf that I didn't stop to realize I should've called for help.

"I'm such a fucking moron..." I muttered, swiping a hand over my eyes in exasperation. I stood there for a while, feeling like a total idiot as the weight of my situation came crashing down on me.

I abandoned my boyfriend after hitting him to chase a wolf into the Shrouded Wood, barefoot and with nothing more than my dad's cloak and a lantern. And for what? The hope that the woman from my dreams was real?

Tears threatened to escape me as I stood there in the middle of the forest. I felt more alone than ever in that moment and feared a full-on nervous breakdown would overwhelm me.

Rosetta...

I gasped as the voice from my dreams called out to me. Her voice seemed stronger somehow, almost *closer*.

Swinging the lantern around to light the area, I searched for the source of the voice. I heard rustling from within the body of trees and aimed the lantern toward them, my eyes widening as the wolf stood, in all of her glory, in the beam's light.

"You're back," I said, unsure of what else to do.

I will always come back for you, Rosetta.

My breath caught in my throat, shock paralyzing me. I stared at the wolf in awe, watching as she took a few steps closer to me from out of the shadows.

"What...?" I found my voice, swallowing thickly as I fought for the right words. "Was that... you? In my head?"

Yes, the voice spoke again. *I told you we were connected now. I meant it.*

"But... how?" I questioned. My eyes widened further as I reached up to touch the scratches over my heart. "It was you, wasn't it? That marked me? Just like my gran said..."

I did, she said. *I marked you. And by doing so, I am able to speak to you in your mind.*

"But why?" I asked. "Why would you mark me?"

She was silent for a moment, her eyes trained directly on me. I felt naked under her gaze, exposed. A chill ran down my spine as I waited for her to answer me.

I've watched you, she finally said. *I have seen you on your way to your grandmother's many times.*

"You've been watching me?" I gasped, my voice sounding flustered and distant.

I had never been as bewitched by someone before as I was... as I am... with you.

My heart thudded wildly in my chest, my grip tightening on the lantern's handle.

"*I* have bewitched *you*?" I asked incredulously.

Unimaginably so... She moved closer to me, her eyes twinkling with mischief. I realized I should have taken a step back, moved as far away from the female wolf as possible, but I didn't. I was fighting the urge to step *closer*.

"So, what?" I said, pulling the top of my corset down with my free hand to expose the scars. "You marked me, for what? To *claim* me?"

A low growl rumbled in the back of her throat as she spoke.

It's the way of my kind, she explained gruffly. *It is the only way for us to connect.*

"Connect in what way?" I asked. "You keep saying we're connected… but how? In what way are we connected?"

I can communicate with you, she said.

"But there's more to it than that," I accused. "You've done something to me, *changed* me, haven't you? All of these strange feelings I've been having…" I paused, considering everything that had happened to me since she scratched me. "And the cut on my forehead. It healed incredibly quick, because of *you*."

She was quiet for a moment, her ears flickering as she seemed to be mulling over her words carefully.

Yes, I have changed you.

"You admit it."

I will not lie to you, Rosetta, she said gently. *I indeed changed you, marked you,* claimed *you. But, let me ask you this…*

"Yes?" I urged.

Do you resent me for it?

I opened my mouth to speak, but then stopped and closed it. Her question threw me off guard, not because of what it was, but because of the answer that undoubtedly popped in my head.

"No," I said quietly. "I don't resent you."

You're strong willed, she said. *You fight because it's in your nature. But, for just this once... why don't you give in to your true desires?*

I watched as the wolf's form shuddered, her sandy brown fur standing on end as she closed her eyes and inhaled a deep breath. The fur along the slope of her back began to shrink into her body, her four legs shifting as her paws began to expand and lengthen into fingers, an extra toe sprouting forth to form the thumb on each hand. Her tail sunk into her rear, disappearing completely. Her snout began to flatten against her face, her ears shrinking into the normal shape of human ears. As her hind legs began to lengthen and reshape themselves, she stood tall on them to expose the small, white tuft of fur on her stomach that I hadn't seen before. It too shrunk into her body, revealing smooth skin underneath.

I marveled as the wolf transformed in front of my eyes, dropping the lantern to the ground in surprise, the light spreading without my having to hold it up. She shed the form of a wolf and took on the appearance of *her*.

The woman from my dreams.

A quick intake of breath was all I could manage as I took in her appearance. "You're so beautiful," I whispered, staring at every inch of her. And she was... breathtakingly gorgeous.

I marveled at her long, blonde hair, which seemed appropriate considering her fur was a sandy color. The locks were straight and came down below her hips in what seemed like beautiful beams of sunshine. Her slender body was bare, standing before me with confidence and authority, as if she were possibly some sort of royalty among her kind.

To touch her in that moment would've been the epitome of pleasure. Seeing her stand before me in such a vulnerable state, yet so poised all in the same breath, made her even more attractive in my eyes.

With slow, measured steps, she approached me, her movements so graceful and fluid, as if she were floating on air. The atmosphere between us had a charge to it, an energy that strengthened our bond somehow, and made a series of tingles explore every surface of my skin. The connection between us seemed so much stronger now that we were together in the waking world rather than in my dreams.

Aching to touch her soft skin, I raised my hand toward her, but then hesitated. Was it okay for me to touch her? After all, she did just transform from being a wolf to... to a beautiful woman. I'd only ever touched her in my dreams, and even then, she was the one to initiate contact. Yet, my fingers tingled at just the thought of joining with her cheek—skin on skin.

Noticing my hesitation, she nodded, adding a smile to her words as she said, "Go ahead. I don't bite." The quip didn't go unnoticed.

Following her acceptance, I tentatively closed the distance and pressed my palm to her cheek, cupping her stunning face in my hand. The jolt of pleasure that seeped through to my heart increased as she closed her eyes and leaned further into my touch, telling me she enjoyed it as much as I did.

With butterflies filling my stomach, I took one step closer so our bodies were nearly touching, my thumb tracing a light path along the corner of her mouth and across her bottom lip.

Opening her eyes, she looked at me with lust and adoration in her gaze. The color of her irises was both shocking and mesmerizing, making me wish I could spend eternity staring into their depths.

"My, your eyes are such a stunning color of gold," I admired, staring into them with the utmost reverence and amazement.

"Better to look upon your beauty with, Rosetta," she answered, fluttering her lashes as her eyes rolled and closed, continuing to enjoy my thumb tracing the ridge of her mouth. The rich, red color of her lips had my gaze following the path of my thumb in pure, spellbinding hunger.

"And your lips, they're so amazingly soft and plump," I revered, continuing to feather my touch over the smooth, plush surface.

"Better to taste you with as I kiss you," she explained, never taking her eyes off me as I sustained caressing her with both my fingers and my stare.

Bringing her hand up to lay on top of mine, I noticed those stunning claws adorning her fingers—the same ones I admired in my dream—the same ones that looked so sinfully amazing against my skin. They were long, sharp, and simply stunning.

"And I just love how your claws match my scars," I said, taking her hand in mine and placing light kisses against her knuckles, fingers, and everywhere else I could manage to put my lips.

"Better to feel you with, to trace along your skin, and to make you writhe with pleasure beneath me, my dear," she said in a near whisper, her body now flush up against mine. Heat radiated between us as we stood in the middle of the Shrouded Wood, her naked and me just dying to get my clothes off too, so there'd be nothing between our hearts but flesh.

Without another word spoken between us, she closed the distance, her kiss filled with a passion no simple words could express. I matched her vigor as my fingers tangled in her hair, worried that if I let go, it would end way too soon.

"Ahh," I cried out between breaths, the claw marks on my chest burning as our tongues tangled together, igniting a fire deep inside me at the mere touch of this woman—so stunning, so sensual.

"I want you to stay with me," she panted, her breaths just as ragged as mine, our lips still locked in a heated passion one only finds in a romance flick. Her words echoing in my mind had me slowing, pulling away to catch my breath as I contemplated her words. There was only one answer I could give her—one answer that wouldn't make my heart break in two—one answer that would keep me whole.

"Yes," I whispered, looking into her eyes to make sure she heard the quiet, one-syllable word that meant more than the world. The joy in her eyes told me it was the answer she'd been hoping for all along. All I could do was lay my head on her shoulder, as if a huge weight had been lifted off mine, and I suddenly felt free to be me.

Standing in each other's arms, staring up at the full moon lighting up the sky, I wondered what would come next for us. How would we make this… arrangement… work?

As if I spoke the question out loud, she caressed my hair and said, "Don't you worry. Things have a way of working themselves out."

"But why me?" I blurted, looking into her eyes for some sort of sincerity, some way of knowing that I was worthy. "What's so special about me?"

Her gaze bore into my soul, each little flick of her eyes telling me she was examining every aspect of my face as I asked those all-important words. Her features softened as she spoke and said, "Oh, Rosetta, I've been waiting so long, just for the right time to be with you."

"But why?" I repeated. "Why me? There are so many others…"

She placed a clawed finger gently against my lips to silence me. "Hush, darling," she whispered tenderly. "You are the one I choose. I know there are others that I could have, but I don't want them. I want *you*."

I felt my insides nearly melt at her words. Leaning up, I captured her lips again, my stomach twisting in knots as an unimaginable amount of joy filled me. My skin felt hot as I touched her, my fingers dancing over her biceps. She reciprocated the kiss, holding me tight as if I were going to run away. How could I possibly even think of running away from her?

It was then that I realized that my skin was growing even hotter, more so than was comfortable. I pulled back from her, a gasp leaving my lungs in a huff, the knot in my stomach revealing itself to be more than just butterflies as it throbbed, feeling a strange sensation radiate throughout my body. I looked into her eyes, questioning, pleading for some answers.

"It'll be okay, my beloved Rosetta," she said soothingly. "This will be the worst that it'll ever be. It'll become easier, more comfortable as you grow into it."

I tried to pull away from her, but she held me tight against her, not letting me go. I began to hyperventilate, the air around me growing thick, stifling my labored breaths.

"W-what's happening?"

"I told you that things have a way of working themselves out," she explained, a sad smile adorning her face as I writhed in her arms. "This is the only way."

A soft groan trembled from my lips as the bones of my fingers crackled. I lifted my hands to watch as the fingernails of my four top digits began to sharpen, growing longer until a set of claws glinted in the lantern's light. My thumbs began to shrivel, as if they were balloons being deflated, the palms of my hands hardening into pads.

"The moon is the catalyst," she said, taking my now-clawed hand into her own. I marveled at how similar we were now, our fingers intertwining. "You will not be controlled by it, but merely *strengthened* by it. It's why I had to wait so dreadfully long to come to you. I had to wait for the moon to come."

Little hairs began to grow along my arms, just a shade darker than the strands atop my head. My pants became more ragged as I felt something poke at my lips. Running my tongue over my teeth, I discovered that my canines had elongated into sharp fangs.

"The moon has reached its apex," she continued. I realized then that she was talking to try and help calm me. The look on her face was that of guilt, as if my pain caused her pain. "It'll be over soon, I promise."

She stroked my hair, and I closed my eyes, focusing on it—focusing on *her*. She held me tight, whispering sweet nothings as I felt my body change. The muscles along my back shifted, forcing me to crouch onto the ground. Following, she never once let me go as I groaned and cried. She placed kisses against my forehead, even after it was covered in fur and my face had distended forward. Cradling me in her arms, she gently pulled away my clothing as my body didn't fit in them anymore. She smiled as I stopped whimpering and looked up at her, the world around us seemingly different from behind my new eyes.

"You're just as beautiful in the form of a wolf as you are a human, Rosetta," she said, leaning forward to place a kiss on my snout.

I tried to speak, but found my vocal chords weren't meant for human speech. I whined, not out of discomfort, but because I couldn't express to her how much I wanted to be able to kiss her back.

"It's okay, my darling," she said in response to my thoughts. "Let me join you."

Her transformation was quicker than mine, I noticed, as I watched her revert back to the wolf. She didn't once groan or cry out as she changed, reminding me of how she said it would get easier with time. Once she was done, she stood tall with her sandy brown fur and glowing, golden eyes. I felt awkward walking on four legs, but I did my best to step forward and rub my head against her soft mane, reveling in her scent that washed over me. She licked my ear, and I shivered with delight as we twined together to share auras.

I'd never felt so complete before, my life always seeming to be missing something important, though I could never figure out what. Now, standing here in the form of a wolf along with my mate, I felt whole, like I'd been waiting a lifetime to find this kind of fulfillment and acceptance.

Rosetta, my love, her voice echoed in my mind, filling me with adoration and joy. *Catch me.*

Without waiting for my response, she turned and ran off into the Shrouded Wood. I was reminded of when she appeared to me at the river, teasing me with her gaze and her game of cat and mouse. She was doing the same now.

And like before, I didn't hesitate to run after her.

THE END OF

†EMP†

BOOK ONE IN THE
TWISTED WOLF TALES SERIES

Continue on with more unique retellings of classic
fairy tales with the Twisted Wolf Tales Series.
Release information can be found on Rene's website
at www.renefolsom/twisted-wolf-tales.

In the meantime,
here's a sneak peek of what's to come next:

TRUST

A TWISTED WOLF TALE

Beau Shapiro has spent his whole life being called gorgeous, handsome, sexy... every word imaginable to describe his outer appearance. But despite his popularity, he never once lets it all go to his head. He's holding out for that one girl that has it all—beauty *and* personality.

While out searching for his father, Beau meets Karoline—a woman cursed to be a beast. Striking a deal with her to save his father's life, Beau is taken to Karoline's home deep in the mountainous woods to live with her. During his stay, he finds that there's beauty within the beast, and slowly, for the first time in his life, falls in love.

Delve into the story of Beau and Karoline, a modern day retelling of the classic tale *Beauty and the Beast*.

Warning: This supernatural romance novella contains adult situations and is meant for ages 18+.

Find out more on Rene's website at
http://renefolsom.com/trust

THE RED HOT TREATS
COLLECTION

This Halloween, something sinfully wicked is coming your way. Give yourself a Red Hot Treat this fall with ten spine-tingling stories sure to warm up your night. Scary just got sexy with TEMPT, part of the Red Hot Treats multi-author series of nine stories for 99 cents each. Each book stands alone for reading enjoyment.

For more spooky Halloween fun, check out these other stories and get your *treat* on!

www.redhotauthors.com

Kissin' Hell by Jodi Redford

There are two certainties in life soul collector and hellhound Jericho Stryker knows too well—Death never takes a holiday, and women are typically more trouble than they're worth. That goes double for his personal nemesis and regular pain in his backside, Lola McKenna. Sure, the luscious little hellcat gets his blood boiling in more ways than one, but some scratches are best left un-itched. That determination is strained to the max when a botched soul acquisition job lands him on the same case as Lola.

Fetching a stubborn soul from a haunted bordello should be a piece of cake. Unfortunately for Lola, she has to deal with Jericho horning in on her bounty. Attempting to keep her cool and her wits around her sinfully sexy adversary? Easier said than done. Especially when she finds herself locked overnight with Jericho. Not strangling him before sunrise? A faint possibility. Ignoring the lusty, depraved sexual fantasies he awakens in her? A snowball's chance in hell of happening. But worst of all is the very real possibility that he could steal the one thing she most fears losing to him—her heart.

www.jodiredford.com/That_Old_Black_Magic.html

Eyes of the Wolf by Desiree Holt

When Jamie Dalton moved into the mouse her grandparents left her she was just looking to reconnect with her past and settle in familiar surroundings. Digging through the attic for treasures, she found a nearly life-sized statue of a wolf and a very old, very strange book, Legends of the Werewolf. Each night after returning home from her job as the town's head librarian, she curled up in a big chair with her little black cat, Mischief, fascinated by what she read. She was shocked when her new neighbor, Mike Volka, introduced himself and the eyes watching her looked just like the wolf in the book.

Mike Volka's ancestors once owned Jamie's house and the book that is his heritage as a wolf shifter, the one that will guide his future, is hidden somewhere inside. He sure didn't expect the intense sexual heat the erupted between them. When he sneaks into her house and sees her asleep in the big chair, the book open on her lap, the temptation to have her is too great for him. Using the hypnotic power of the shifter, he draws her into his web and they have sex so hot it nearly burns down the house.

But can a union born in stealth survive? Is she the human mate his family had told him might be waiting for him? Will Jamie succumb to his hot alpha impact and can she believe what others dismiss as a fanciful legend? On Halloween night it will come to an explosive conclusion but will the heat consume them or bind them closer together.

www.desireeholt.com

All Flash No Cash by **Randi Alexander**

When Deadwood, South Dakota bar owner CJ Overton hires Pete Gonally to paint a motorcycle for a charity giveaway, she expects him to do it her way. After all, he's a small-time rancher, and graphic arts is just his hobby. But Pete comes back with his own ideas, and sparks fly as tension builds between them. The only way to relieve the pressure is one hot night in her bed. Just one. But then Pete wants more.

Pete lets CJ think he's just a farm boy, but working on the oil field for years, he's accumulated a small fortune; more than enough capital to buy his family ranch plus thousands of acres surrounding it. CJ's dream future includes selling the bar, leaving Deadwood, and traveling the world. Attaching herself to a hayseed like Pete would only ruin her chances. How can Pete convince CJ that falling for a "dirt-poor farmer" will make her happier than anything she'd ever find outside of South Dakota?

www.randialexander.com/preview/red-hot-treats-flash-cash/

Tribulation Road by Shyla Colt

The members of Noble exist in the shadows, keeping the evil seeking to ruin the world at bay. For centuries, the covert organization caused fear in the hearts of the supernatural community. But that is all about to change. As the daughter of the Noble Clan leader, Brigh Howell is prepared for anything. Until one hunt changes life as she knows it.

With the revelation of a betrayer in the ranks, she's forced to call the one man she hoped she would never see again. Her ex-fiancée and Noble deserter, Jaeger Sutton.

Forced to work together to save their clan, the two find the connection between them is still alive and well. Will airing their secrets be enough to mend the broken pieces of what once was?

www.shylacolt.com

Hot Caramel Passion by Graylin Rane

Ava's skills as a chef took her from private celebrity chef to owner of Miami's hottest new restaurant. Shy since kindergarten, she expressed her passions in the kitchen. Loneliness lowered her shoulders as the accolades faded at closing each night. At thirty-three, she was still single, preferring a crowded kitchen to a man across a small table.

Her brother signed her up with Viviana, owner of The Candy Man Delivery Service. She'd been appalled until he showed her the picture of Viviana's man, Adonis. Her anxiety quelled each day by a furious work schedule then ran rampant over her mind as she tried to sleep.

Exhausted and shaking, she opens her condo door to find Marcus with caramel colored skin, dark hair, and intense brown eyes. He helps her bloom as she experiences complete devotion for the first time in her life.

www.graylinfox.com/candy-man-delivery-service-stories/hot-caramel-passion/

Love's Magic Spell By Sable Hunter and Ryan O'Leary

Tory has one magical night to learn what love is all about.

Night after lonely night, she tosses in her solitary bed, longing to touch and be touched, to experience desire and rapture. Her body aches to know fulfillment –to be taken and possessed by a man, but only one man will do.

Raylan West is the man of her dreams and Tory Summers would give everything she owns for a chance with him. But it isn't going to happen, a man like him is not for her. Unless…Tori finds a way. Deep in the bayous of South Louisiana there are secrets, magical secrets. Hoodoo. Witchcraft. Will o' the wisp floating over dark waters, lit by unearthly light.

Desperate for a chance, Tory places her faith in the supernatural. She travels deep into the swamp to acquire a love potion promised to bring Raylan under her spell for one night, one perfect moonlit Halloween night where anything is possible. For a few precious hours, Tory will be beautiful, desirable and sexy in Raylan's eyes.

The only problem is…Tori wants the magic to last forever.

www.sablehunter.com

Mask of Fire by **Michel Prince**

Barton Nuril has attended the Harvester's Gala for more years than most. He'd given up the dream that a woman would want him for more than copulation until a dark haired beauty he dubs Firefights to get him in bed. Even as those from his province plot to take down the establishment and all its traditions, Barton for once, is discovering love may exist.

Abigail Stone knew the Rules chapter and verse. Even as others perverted their purpose, Abby stayed true and attended the Harvester's Gala to find her soulmate. Just as she feels she's found him the fates step in between omens and a battle no one could have foretold Abby is sure her choice is doomed. Will she see beyond her traditions and still stay within the rules to find love?

Can love ignite when one believes it no longer exists and the other fears the fates have doomed the union?

www.MichelPrinceBooks.com

Cat on the Prowl by Sandy Sullivan

Suzi is on the run from something or someone, she isn't quite sure. Mitchell Cruz wants her dead if he can't have her. His plan to dispose of her body in the middle of the dense forest seemed like he perfect way to make her disappear without a trace until she manages to cold cock him with a branch and get away.

In her mad dash to safety, she stumbles across a lone cabin with an inviting light drawing her near. Hoping to find an elderly couple to give her shelter until she can find a way out, she knocks at the door to be met by only silence except for the rumbling growl of a mountain lion in the distance.

Gabriel is a shifter. Suzi is his mate and he's bound by the laws of love to save her from the evil clutches of a wolf shifter intending on doing her harm. When she stumbles upon his cabin, he knows fate has brought her to him finally in her hour of need.

Can a shifter and a human find love amongst the tall trees, mountainous streams and softly falling snow?

www.romancestorytime.com

ABOUT RENE

Rene Folsom, author of paranormal romance and erotica, lives in Florida with her husband and three kids. She has officially diagnosed herself with creative ADD and often has a million and one writing projects going at once. In addition to writing, she is also a graphic artist who enjoys creating custom book covers for indie authors. She is definitely an artist at heart and would love nothing more than to be elbow deep in clay during her waking hours.

Rene believes that all fiction is based on some form of reality—otherwise we would never have the inspiration or knowledge to dream up the realistic situations we portray with our words. She is proud to say that her personal experiences have been inspirational, though perhaps not always identical to that of her fictional characters. Where reality and fantasy diverge, however, must remain her little secret...

FOLLOW RENE

Newsletter
www.renefolsom.com/newsletter

Website
www.renefolsom.com

Facebook
www.facebook.com/renefolsom

Goodreads
www.goodreads.com/renefolsom

Amazon
www.amazon.com/author/renefolsom

BOOKS BY RENE

Cornerstone Series

Shuttered Affections & Exposed Affections

www.ReneFolsom.com/cornerstone

Roommate Romance Series

Heart You, Bind Me, Share You, & Flatter Me
(also available in a boxed set)

www.ReneFolsom.com/roommates

Soul Seers Series

Voices of the Soul, Eyes of the Soul,
Truths of the Soul, Blood of the Soul,
Secrets of the Soul, & Hearts of the Soul
(also available in a boxed set)

www.ReneFolsom.com/soulseers

Favorite Things Series
(co-written with Juli Valenti)

Adventurous & Bound
(more titles coming soon)

www.ReneFolsom.com/favorite-things

Standalones

Every Thorn (A Romantic Thriller Short Story)
www.ReneFolsom.com/everythorn

Have My Heart (A Romantic Short Story)
www.ReneFolsom.com/hmh

Red Hot Authors Collections

For Liberty: A Red Hot and BOOM! Story
Tempt: A Red Hot Treats Story

www.ReneFolsom.com/redhot

Anthologies

Paranormal Anthology with a Twist
Stalkers: A Collection of Thriller Stories
Stardust: A Futuristic Romance Collection
All Our Love: A Collection of Romance Stories

www.ReneFolsom.com/label/anthologies

Made in the USA
San Bernardino, CA
16 January 2016